D1452177

Mikaeel and Malaika
The Power of Dua

Written by: Kazima Wajahat

Copyright © 2020 Kazima Wajahat
All rights reserved. No part of this book may be reproduced or transmitted in any form
or by any means, electronic or mechanical, including photocopying, recording, or by any
information storage and retrieval system, without written permission from the publisher.
For permission requests, contact publisher.
ISBN: 978-0-578-63348-0
Printed and bound in China
Books by Kazima Wajahat are available at special discounts when purchased in quantity
for premiums and promotions as well as
fundraising or educational use.
For details, contact: info@flowersofmygarden.com

All praise to the One who has blessed me with the most selfless and unconditionally supportive
family I could have ever prayed for.
Don't know where I would be without y'all Baba, Mummy, AA, QHA, ZFA, KAR, and TZW.
A very special thanks to HFR, NS, EH.

Mikaeel and Malaika were brother and sister and they both had one thing in common.

They were superheroes.

At least they used to be.

One day, as they were walking back from the masjid after Jummah prayer, they heard:

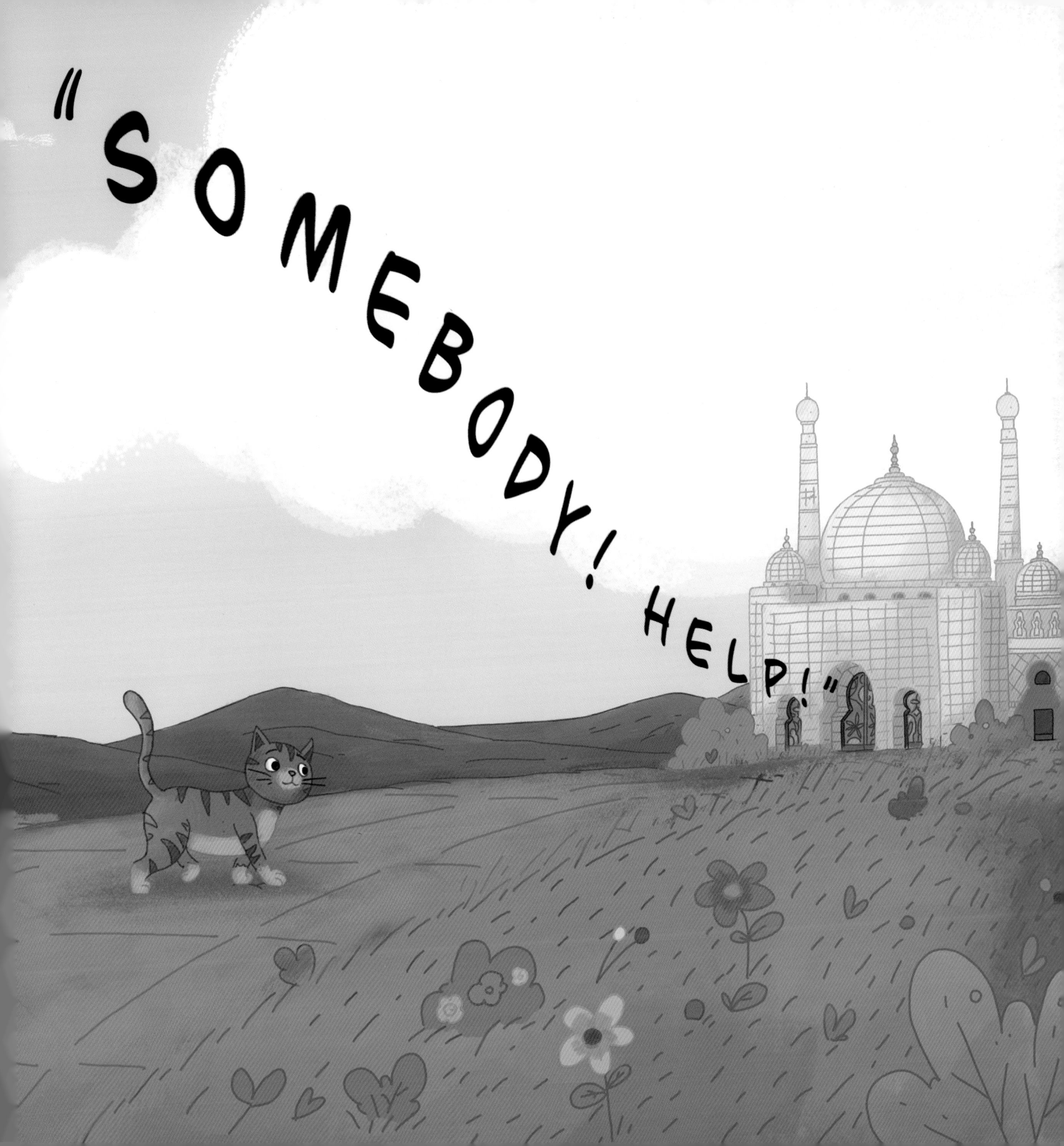
"SOMEBODY! HELP!"

Mikaeel and Malaika glanced at each other and quickly whipped on their capes and rushed to the scene of the crime. It was time for another mission.

"What happened Sister Sarah?"

"Someone has taken all our shoes!" she wailed.

"Don't worry. We'll get to the bottom of this," Mikaeel reassured her.

The superheroes ran to the parking lot, raised both hands to the sky, jumped into the air and-

fell back down.

They tried again.

Arms outstretched, they sprung off one leg and-

collided with the ground.

"Malaika, our superpowers!" said Mikaeel.

"Why can't we fly anymore?" cried Malaika.

They needed answers. They needed Big Boss.

Big Boss was in the middle of a classified utensil purification process.

"Big Boss, our powers! They're gone!" cried Mikaeel.

"Alas, my superheroes. Your superhero lifestyle was only a 14 day free trial."

"Free trial?" Mikaeel and Malaika were shocked.

"No powers? No problem!" exclaimed Mikaeel.

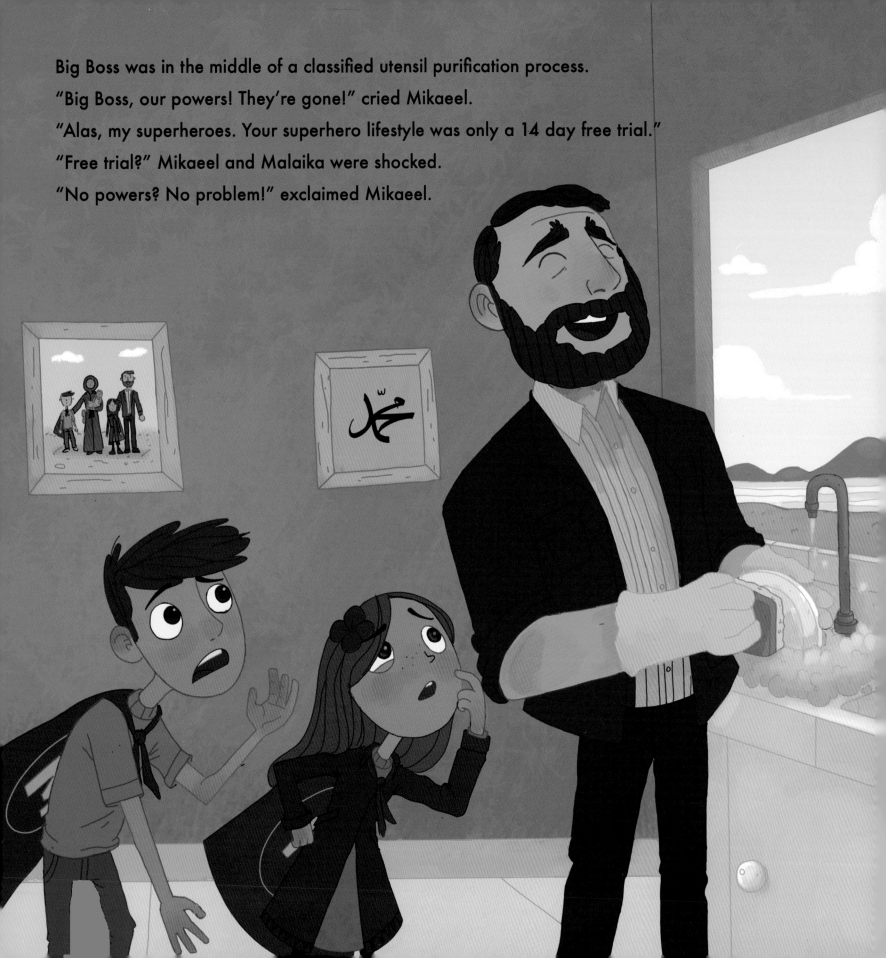

"We still have...."

Mikaeel opened his super secret garage.

"Our......"

"....superjet? It's GONE!"

Mikaeel and Malaika ran back to Command Post.

Big Boss was skimming through a high profile superhero manual.

"Big Boss, our superjet! It's gone!" cried Mikaeel

"Oh that old thing you flew on?

I sold that on Spamazon." Big Boss chuckled.

Mikaeel and Malaika were lost.
"No super powers? No super jet?
What about Mission: Disappearing
Shoes?"asked Mikaeel.
Big Boss laughed.
"My superheroes, there is no need for your
distress. There is one superpower you still
possess."

Mikaeel jumped.

"Oh! I still have my super
X-ray vision?"

Big Boss shook his head.

"Super speed?"

"Not quite..."

"Super strength?"

"No..."

"Super meal consumption?"

Big Boss raised an eyebrow.

"What? I get hungry," shrugged Mikaeel.

"The power of Dua is your greatest strength.
Asking Allah will take you to great lengths."
"The power of dua?" asked Malaika.
"YES! The power of dua!" Mikaeel and Malaika exclaimed running to their prayer mat.

"Oh Allah, you are the Most Merciful, the All Powerful.
Please help us find the missing shoes."
Mikaeel and Malaika finished their dua and waited.
And waited.
And waited some more.
"Let's go check now!"

They checked the shelves. No shoes.

They checked inside. No shoes.

They checked outside. Still no shoes.

So, the superheroes headed back to Command Post.

Big Boss was busy sanitizing the infantile waste unit.

"Big Boss, we've lost all our powers. Even our power of dua.

The shoes are still missing!" cried Mikaeel.

"Have patience my son,

for an apple is only good to eat,

when it has turned red, ripe, and sweet."

Mikaeel and Malaika hitched a ride with
Grandpa to the apple orchard.
"Oh Allah, you are the Most Loving, the Giving.
Please, please help us find the missing shoes."

Mikaeel grabbed a small green apple from the tree.

"Mikaeel! Wait!!!"

"Blegh! That was so sour."

Malaika stopped and thought.

"An apple is only good to eat when it has turned red, ripe, and sweet."

Malaika handed Mikaeel a bright red apple.

"Try this one."

"Mmm.. sweet!"

Mikaeel and Malaika returned to Command Post.

"Big Boss, any news on the shoes?" questioned Mikaeel.

Big Boss was training the new superhero recruit.

"Patience my son,

for a caterpillar will never fly

if it doesn't wait to become a butterfly."

Mikaeel and Malaika raised their hands in the middle of the butterfly garden.
"Oh Allah, you are the All Knowing, the All Aware.
Please, please, pleasseeee help us find the missing shoes."

"Mikaeel, a caterpillar!"
Mikaeel stroked the tiny green caterpillar.
"But why isn't it flying?" he wondered.

Malaika stopped and thought.
"A caterpillar will never fly
if it doesn't wait to become a butterfly."

"Look, the cocoon. It's moving!" Malaika pointed.
Bit by bit, the cocoon began to shed.

Out blossomed a beautiful butterfly.
Mikaeel and Malaika watched in awe.

Mikaeel and Malaika returned to Command Post.

Big Boss was concocting his infamous superhero nourishment biscuits.

Mikaeel sat at the table and reached for one.

"Patience, my superhero. Rewards are best when the time is -"

"I'm tired of waiting! I've been waiting and praying for days and my dua won't come true! Why oh why won't my dua come true?"

Mikaeel interrupted.

"Mikaeel! Rewards are best when the time is right.
Rewards will come with Allah's might.
Allah gives us ripe red apples to eat
but only when we wait for them to be sweet.
Only by waiting will a caterpillar fly by turning into a butterfly,"
exclaimed Malaika.
'And don't forget to ask Allah. He loves when we ask Him and do dua,"
said Big Boss

That night, after Maghrib prayer, Mikaeel and Malaika raised their hands in dua again.

"Oh Allah, you are the All Seeing, the All Hearing, the Just.

Please help us find the missing shoes, but only when You feel we must."

"Mikaeel! Malaika! Come outside!" called Super Agent M.O.M.

Mikaeel and Malaika couldn't believe their eyes.
Behind the masjid, under the bushes were fluffy newborn kittens
keeping warm in none other than the missing shoes.

Allah had made their dua come true.
Mikaeel smiled and said,
"Thank you Allah."
"Rewards will come with Allah's might.
Rewards are best when the time is right."

"When My devotees enquire of you about Me, I am near, and answer the call of every supplicant when he calls. It behoves them to hearken to Me and believe in Me that they may follow the right path."

The Holy Quran 2:186